BE AN EFFECTIVE COMMUNICATOR

READING BODY LANGUAGE

AMY B. ROGERS

New York

Published in 2022 by The Rosen Publishing Group, Inc.
29 East 21st Street, New York, NY 10010

Copyright © 2022 by The Rosen Publishing Group, Inc.

First Edition

Portions of this work were originally authored by Liz Sonneborn and published as *Nonverbal Communication: The Art of Body Language*. All new material in this edition authored by Amy B. Rogers.

All rights reserved. No part of this book may be reproduced in any form without permission in writing from the publisher, except by a reviewer.

Library of Congress Cataloging-in-Publication Data

Names: Rogers, Amy B., author.
Title: Reading body language / Amy B. Rogers.
Description: New York : Rosen Publishing, [2022] | Series: Be an effective communicator | Includes bibliographical references and index.
Identifiers: LCCN 2021029094 (print) | LCCN 2021029095 (ebook) | ISBN 9781499470260 (library binding) | ISBN 9781499470253 (paperback) | ISBN 9781499470277 (ebook)
Subjects: LCSH: Body language.
Classification: LCC BF637.N66 R64 2022 (print) | LCC BF637.N66 (ebook) | DDC 153.6/9--dc23
LC record available at https://lccn.loc.gov/2021029094
LC ebook record available at https://lccn.loc.gov/2021029095

Manufactured in the United States of America

Some of the images in this book illustrate individuals who are models. The depictions do not imply actual situations or events.

CPSIA Compliance Information: Batch #CWRYA22. For further information, contact Rosen Publishing, New York, New York, at 1-800-237-9932.

CONTENTS

INTRODUCTION — 4

CHAPTER 1
BODY LANGUAGE BASICS — 8

CHAPTER 2
EXAMINING FACIAL EXPRESSIONS — 20

CHAPTER 3
A HANDY COMMUNICATION TOOL — 32

CHAPTER 4
PUTTING THE PIECES TOGETHER — 44

CHAPTER 5
BODY LANGUAGE IN ACTION — 58

GLOSSARY — 70

FOR MORE INFORMATION — 72

FOR FURTHER READING — 74

INDEX — 76

INTRODUCTION

Some people have a way with words. They speak or write well, and some might think this alone makes them very effective communicators—people who can successfully share their thoughts, ideas, and feelings with others and understand the thoughts, ideas, and feelings of others in return. However, words are only one tool we use when we communicate.

Speaking—also known as verbal communication—is an important part of how we express ourselves and how others express themselves to us. For example, if you want to tell a potential boss in a job interview that they should hire you, you might say, "I think I'd be the perfect fit for this position." In a similar way, if you ask how a friend is doing and they say, "I'm doing great," you'd most likely assume they're having a good day.

Words don't always tell the whole story, though. If you tell a potential boss, "I think I'd be a perfect fit for this position," but you won't make eye contact with them and you're slouching in your chair, they might not believe your words. The same thing could happen if your friend tells you

Effective communicators know the words we use are only one of the many ways we communicate at home, at school, and at work.

they're doing great but they're frowning and their body is turned away from you. Would you still think they're having a good day?

Nonverbal communication, which is the way we express thoughts and feelings without words, can often tell us just as much as—and sometimes more than—verbal communication. One of the most important aspects of nonverbal communication is body language, or the ways we communicate through the movement of our body.

Without even knowing it, we communicate so much through our body language every day. When we slowly walk into the kitchen for breakfast without making eye contact with anyone else, we're communicating that we're tired and don't want to talk yet. When we move our hands a lot while telling a story, we're communicating that we're excited. Even the way we stand tells a story. Standing up tall and taking up space lets people know we feel confident, while slouching and looking down at our feet makes us look shy or sad.

Body language involves the facial expressions we make, the gestures we use, our posture, and much more. Each of those things plays an important part in the messages we send out to others and the messages they send out to us. However, it's not always easy to interpret someone else's body language, and we sometimes communicate things with our own body language that we don't want to or don't mean to. This is why having a deep understanding of body language is such an important part of being an effective communicator. It allows us

INTRODUCTION

Body language includes the position of our body when we speak and when we're listening. Leaning in shows we're paying attention.

to examine our own behavior more closely so we can more clearly communicate exactly what we want to share with others. It also allows us to develop a stronger understanding of the people we're communicating with and the things they're saying without words.

Nonverbal communication has helped humans connect throughout history and across language barriers. Taking a closer look at what body language is and what it commonly communicates can help us strengthen our connections to others, avoid miscommunication and misunderstandings, and be sure others are seeing us exactly as we want to be seen.

CHAPTER 1

BODY LANGUAGE BASICS

A deeper understanding of body language starts with the most basic question: What is it? Body language involves nearly every body part—from head to toe, literally. Facial expressions and head movements are key parts of our body language, and even the positioning of our legs and feet can communicate how we're feeling. Body language also includes eye contact, hand movements, and even the amount of space between people in a conversation.

With so many different aspects of body language to look at, you might think it's been studied for many years and in great depth. However, it's still a relatively new field of study. In 1872, the renowned naturalist Charles Darwin (who proposed the theory of evolution), published *The Expression of the Emotions in Man and Animals*. In this work, Darwin discussed the similarities in facial expressions among humans, apes, and monkeys, all of which, according to his theory, evolved from a common ancestor. For many years, this early study in nonverbal communication remained one of the few scholarly books on the subject of body language.

It took until the middle of the 20th century for scientists and other scholars to begin considering body language as a serious subject worthy of further study. Since then, it's been a major topic of research among scientists in many different areas, including zoology (the study of animals), anthropology (the study of human beings in relation to one another), and psychology (the study of the human mind and human behavior).

Technology has even been developed to study body language—specifically facial expressions. The Facial Action Coding System (FACS) was created in the 1970s to analyze facial movements. It's gone through many updates, and it continues to be used to interpret emotions based on facial expressions. It's been used by psychologists to help analyze their patients' emotional states and by animators to help them better depict a full range of emotions in the characters they create.

Body language is still a developing field of study, and it's not always an exact science. However, it's been a part of human communication since the first humans walked the earth, and it's the first way most people learn to express

READING BODY LANGUAGE

Understanding body language is helpful for psychologists, who sometimes work with patients who struggle to verbally express their true feelings.

what they want, need, and feel. As such, it deserves a closer look.

THE EARLIEST FORM OF COMMUNICATION

Before early humans developed spoken language, they were still able to communicate with one another, thanks to body language. They may not have had words, but they had facial expressions and body movements that allowed them to "speak" with those around them.

Even after developing language, humans continued to use movements to express themselves. Nonverbal communication is a part of every interaction we have, and it's especially important when there's a language barrier between people. For example, travelers in a foreign country often have to rely on gestures (such as pointing toward locations or objects), facial expressions, and head movements (such as nodding or shaking their head) to convey information when they're not fully fluent in the language being spoken around them.

Humans use body language from their earliest moments of life. Long before they can speak, babies communicate with their parents through their movements and expressions. Their smiles, frowns, waves, and head movements are able to convey what they're feeling and what they need.

The development of verbal communication skills doesn't make nonverbal communication less important. In fact, it still accounts for a much higher percentage of human communication than spoken words. According to scientific studies conducted in the 1960s, only 7 percent of a message communicated by one person to another comes from the words

READING BODY LANGUAGE

spoken. Tone of voice accounts for 38 percent, while other elements of body language make up 55 percent. Over time, these percentages have been challenged, but researchers generally agree that body language plays a substantial role in any conversation.

Before we learn to talk, we learn to communicate through our faces and our bodies. This baby is smiling to show her mom she is happy to see her.

WHAT WE'RE SAYING AND HOW WE SAY IT:

We know that body language is an important part of communication, but what exactly does it communicate? In general, while words often transmit facts and information, most body language conveys feelings, emotions, and attitudes. This is why words and body language can sometimes conflict. A person might say one thing, but their body language might convey something else. For example, someone might say they're not mad, but their scowl and crossed arms tell a different story.

Communication through body language is almost instant. When you meet strangers, you start forming an opinion about them within seconds, largely because of what they communicate nonverbally. You might see someone who's smiling and standing in a relaxed way and decide they seem friendly. On the other hand, you might meet someone who doesn't look you in the eyes and has their body turned away from the conversation, and you might think they're not looking to make new friends. This can affect how you interact with them.

Experts know that different types of body movements communicate different types of information. In their research, body language experts Paul Ekman and Wallace V. Friesen grouped gestures and other movements into five different categories:

Emblems: These movements take the place of words. For example, putting your index finger to your lips is a way to say "Be quiet" without words.

Illustrators: As their name suggests, these movements help illustrate what you are saying. Unlike emblems, illustrators are used alongside words. An example of an illustrator is forming a big circle with your hands when you say, "I bought a massive cookie at the bakery yesterday!" This illustrates how big the cookie is, complementing what you're saying with words.

Regulators: Regulators help regulate, or control, a conversation. Nodding is often an example of a regulator because it's used to show that a person can continue speaking without interrupting them. Raising a finger or a hand can also serve as a regulator because that can be used to show we'd like a turn in a conversation or that we have a question.

Affect Displays: These movements show a particular emotion. For example, bouncing up and down can convey excitement. Facial expressions are also common examples of affect displays. Affect displays sometimes communicate things without us being aware of what we're doing. We might try to look calm and cool when someone is hurting our feelings, but we often frown or look away without realizing we're showing how upset we really are.

BODY LANGUAGE BASICS

Adaptors: Adaptors help people release nervous tension and relieve anxiety, and they often indicate that a person is not comfortable in their surroundings or with a conversation topic. Rubbing the back of your neck, clicking a pen, and playing with jewelry are all adaptors. Adaptors, like affect displays, are movements we're not always aware we're making.

In the United States, giving someone a thumbs-up is an emblem that shows your approval or encouragement without words.

Different Countries, Different Meanings

People everywhere communicate through body language, and body language is often a helpful tool when speaking with someone from another country who doesn't speak the same language you do. However, in different cultures, the same gesture or body movement can have different meanings.

For instance, in England and France, maintaining eye contact with someone is considered good manners, as it is in the United States. In parts of Africa and Asia, however, it is seen as too aggressive.

Throughout much of the world, nodding suggests you agree with what another person is saying. People in Greece, Iran, and Turkey, though, interpret nodding in the opposite way. If you nod there, you are saying "no."

Many common hand gestures can also get you into trouble abroad. In Nigeria, for example, the standard American hand wave doesn't mean "hello" or "goodbye." Instead, it is an offensive gesture. Similarly, don't congratulate someone in Afghanistan and many Middle Eastern countries on a job well done with a thumbs-up. They will see this as very rude. The "OK" hand gesture is another example of a positive gesture in the United States that's very offensive in some other countries, including many in Latin America.

If you ever plan to travel to a foreign country, you will probably try to learn a little about the language spoken there before you go. Remember, though, that it is just as important to find out about the body language customs in any country you're visiting. Otherwise, you might accidentally confuse or insult the people you meet there.

CAN WE CONTROL IT?

You can't control some of the messages your body sends to others. For instance, feelings of anxiety can cause the pupils of your eyes to dilate, or grow larger. It's a matter of biology. No matter how hard you try, you cannot will your pupils not to dilate in this situation.

When you feel certain emotions, your face will also naturally take on corresponding expressions. When you hear good news, your mouth will form a smile without you having to think about doing it. However, if you want to hide your feelings from others, you have the ability to consciously pull the corners of your mouth down to give your face a more neutral expression. You can also put on a fake smile in an effort to convince others you're happy when you're not. Facial expressions aren't always easy to control, but we do have some degree of power over the emotions we show through our face.

We also sometimes move our bodies without realizing it or consciously controlling it. Adaptors often fall into this category of subconscious body movement. For instance, to comfort yourself in a tense situation, you might bite your nails. When you start doing this, you don't think about doing this action to make you feel more grounded or less anxious. Your decision to bite your nails is made on a purely subconscious level. However, after becoming aware of an adaptor, you can take steps to avoid doing this action. Like facial expressions, it can be hard to consciously change actions that start as subconscious responses, but it can be done.

READING BODY LANGUAGE

On the other hand, some gestures, especially emblems and illustrators, are almost always made consciously. For example, waving goodbye or giving an OK sign with your hand is just as much a conscious act as saying the words "goodbye" or "OK."

Biting your nails is a common adaptor that communicates feelings of anxiety and stress. Other subconscious signals of stress include playing with your hair and tapping your feet.

WHAT CAN IT TEACH US?

Body language is something we have been using since we were babies, and we often use it without even thinking about it. This might make it seem like we don't need to really learn more about it. However, a deeper understanding of body language can help you gain a deeper understanding of the people around you as well as a deeper understanding of yourself and how you show that self to the world.

When we're more aware of what body language is and how it's used, we become more aware of the signals other people are sending through their bodies and what they really mean when they're trying to communicate with us. Understanding body language won't turn you into a mind reader who instantly knows what everyone else is secretly thinking, but it might give you clues about how other people are feeling, which might help you communicate with them better.

Studying body language can also make you more aware of the signals your body is sending—both consciously and subconsciously. It can help you think about how clear your use of emblems, regulators, and illustrators is and what kinds of affect displays and adaptors you use without thinking about them. It can be hard work to use our knowledge of body language to change our nonverbal communication habits. The rewards, though, are worth the effort. You'll have more control over the way others see you and a better sense of awareness about yourself.

EXAMINING FACIAL EXPRESSIONS

We communicate so much through our facial expressions—often without even trying. When we feel a certain emotion, our face is often the first part of our body to show it. This is why closely examining facial expressions—the ones we make and the ones others make around us—is such an important part of studying body language. We can tell a lot about a person from what their face is saying, and our faces often tell others the truth—even when we want to hide it.

People are often more likely to believe what's being communicated through

EXAMINING FACIAL EXPRESSIONS

facial expressions than what our words are saying when the two conflict. For example, Nikki and her best friend, Jamie, have plans to go to the movies on Friday night. However, Nikki asks if she can cancel their plans because the person she has a crush on asked her on a date for that same night. Jamie tells her, "That's fine. I'm happy for you!" Her face, though, is communicating something else. Even though she wants Nikki to believe she's OK with the change in plans, the corners of her mouth turn down just a little, and her eyebrows pull together and lower slightly. Nikki can tell Jamie is upset because of what's being communicated through her facial expression. Being aware of what facial expressions mean and how we use them can help us be better overall communicators and more empathetic people who are aware of the true feelings of those around us.

Facial expressions often give away our real feelings if we're not carefully controlling them. Sometimes people try to hide their faces when they know they can't fake a smile.

UNIVERSAL EMOTIONS AND EXPRESSIONS

Hand gestures often mean different things in different countries. Even head movements like nodding can convey different things to different people. Facial expressions, though, are different. According to the research of psychologist and body language expert Paul Ekman, there are six universal emotions that are expressed through the muscles of the face. Ekman has stated that the facial expressions that accompany these emotions are the same for people all over the world.

No matter where in the world you come from, some facial expressions are universal. Knowing these universal expressions can help us when we communicate with people from other countries.

EXAMINING FACIAL EXPRESSIONS

EMOTION	EXPRESSION
anger	eyebrows pull down and in, forehead wrinkles, nostrils flare, lips tighten
disgust	eyebrows lower, nose wrinkles, upper lip raises
fear	eyebrows raise, upper eyelids lift, mouth opens slightly
happiness	eyes narrow, skin near eyes wrinkles, corners of lips raise, lips separate
sadness	inner end of eyebrows raise, eyelids lower, corners of lips lower
surprise	eyebrows raise, eyes open wide, jaw drops

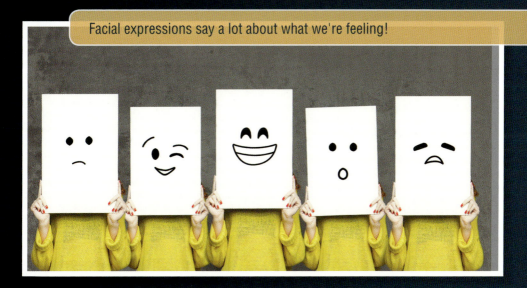

Facial expressions say a lot about what we're feeling!

Ekman later concluded that contempt—expressed by neutral eyes and a half smile on one side of the mouth—is a seventh universal emotion, although some scholars are not convinced that this emotion is recognized by all people. In addition, some scholars have questioned the universality of these emotions and expressions. However, these are still often cited by body language experts as the basis for analyzing facial expressions.

CAN WE REALLY FAKE IT?

When you feel one of these universal emotions, your features tend to automatically move into the corresponding expression. Of course, you can fight that impulse. Everyone knows what it's like to try to look happy when you're sad or to try to hide that you're afraid.

Faking an expression, however, is not always easy. No matter how hard you work at controlling your facial muscles, they sometimes momentarily slip into the expression that reveals your true feelings. These are called microexpressions (sometimes written as micro expressions).

Being aware of microexpressions can help you realize if someone is trying to mask their feelings. It can also help you become more aware of the truths you're showing through your expressions, even if you think you're hiding it well. Also, keep in mind that when someone is faking an emotion, they often get the appropriate facial expression slightly wrong. For example, fake happiness is especially easy to spot. When people put on a fake smile, they often use only the bottom half of their face. The skin on the outer edge of their eyes often doesn't crinkle like it does when a person is smiling sincerely.

A common example of facial expressions giving away the truth is a surprise party for a person who knew it was coming. They often try to act surprised, but if someone was paying close attention, they could probably tell that they were faking it.

SMILES SAY A LOT

A smile is one of the most well-known and comprehensible facial expressions, but not all smiles convey the same meaning. A tight-lipped smile suggests you might be trying to keep something to yourself. Tilting your head down while smiling can mean you're feeling a little embarrassed or shy. A wide smile that lifts your cheeks and reaches your eyes is warm and inviting.

Your mouth gives away your emotions in other ways as well. If you're relaxed, you hold your lips loosely, but if you're tense or anxious, they naturally stretch tight. People also often tighten their lips when they are trying to hide sadness or anger. A sudden puckering of the lips usually signals that someone disagrees with what you're saying. People also sometimes reveal their disapproval by touching their lips or reveal their anxiety by biting them.

THE EYES HAVE IT

Even more revealing than your mouth are your eyes. When you are happy or excited, your eyes seem brighter. When you are sad or bored, they are often blank or unfocused, like you're staring into space.

Eye contact is also an important part of body language. It builds a bond between people and can show confidence and interest in another person. If you're shy, maintaining proper eye contact can be difficult, but with practice, you can often become more comfortable with it. This is important because if you don't look someone in the eyes when speaking to them, they might think you're upset, bored, or distracted, even if you're interested in what they have to say.

On the other hand, unbroken eye contact can make people feel uncomfortable if it goes on for too long. It's often seen as aggressive, especially in certain foreign counties, such as parts of Asia. Finding a balance between too much eye contact and not enough isn't always easy, but once you figure it out, you'll see that it's a great tool to convey friendliness, interest, and respect.

It's good to maintain eye contact while shaking someone's hand. It shows that you're feeling confident and that you're happy to meet them.

ASD and Nonverbal Communication

Some people have a more difficult time understanding and communicating through body language than others. One reason someone might struggle with this is because they have autism spectrum disorder (ASD), which is commonly shortened to autism. There are many signs that someone might have ASD, including not responding to their name, having a lot of trouble expressing their own feelings or understanding other people's feelings, and getting upset over small changes to their routine. Sensory processing difficulties, such as an inability to tolerate certain foods because of their texture, are common among people with ASD too.

Nonverbal communication is an area of difficulty for some people with ASD. For example, making appropriate facial expressions to communicate feelings is something people with ASD sometimes struggle with, as is interpreting others' facial expressions to know what they're feeling. In addition, a possible sign of ASD in babies is not using gestures, such as waving or pointing to things they want, by the time they're 18 months old.

Eye contact can also be difficult for people with ASD. They sometimes avoid looking at other people's eyes or struggle to maintain eye contact for an extended period of time.

People with ASD might have a hard time with some aspects of nonverbal communication, but that doesn't mean other people should avoid communicating with them completely. Instead, treating people with ASD with patience, understanding, and empathy can make them feel welcome and accepted.

USING YOUR HEAD

When talking to someone, facial expressions are important, but the movements of your whole head can also be used to communicate what you're thinking and feeling. From raising your head to indicate interest to nodding your head to say "yes" and shaking your head to say "no," you can say so much if you use your head!

Sometimes people talk with their heads very close together. This head position increases the intimacy between people and sends the signal that they do not want to be interrupted. People with their heads leaned in toward one another are showing each other that they're very interested in the conversation.

Another way to show someone you're interested in what they're saying is by tilting your head. By just slightly tilting your head to one side, you can assure other people that you're actively listening to them. On the other hand, tilting your head backward with your chin jutting forward is a much less friendly gesture. It suggests you think you're better than the other people in the conversation. Tilting your head down with your chin close to your chest conveys the opposite message. It says you are shy or uncomfortable.

When a teacher is talking at school, people often rest their chin in one of their hands. The gesture makes them look extremely bored and tired—so much so that if someone grabbed their hand away, you would expect their head to simply flop forward. As such, if you want others to think they have your full attention, this is not always a good gesture to make. However, as with many aspects of body language, reading head-to-hand contact is not always so simple. If your eyes are bright and focused, lightly resting your hand on your cheek can actually make you look as though you're thinking long and hard about someone's words.

ONLY PART OF THE STORY.

Facial expressions, eye contact, and head movements are important parts of a person's body language. However, there's so much more to nonverbal communication than just what we show from the neck up. Each expression or gesture is like a word—it can have meaning on its own, but it's often used as part of a larger story. It's only when we look at all the aspects of body language put together that we can figure out the story someone else is trying to tell us about themselves.

EXAMINING FACIAL EXPRESSIONS

What do you think the position of this person's head indicates about his attitude? Does he look friendly to you?

CHAPTER 3
A HANDY COMMUNICATION TOOL

A person's face is only one tool they use to communicate. Another important tool is their hands. Some people are known for talking with their hands. They use big, expressive hand gestures when telling a story or making a point. However, everyone who has the ability to do so talks with their hands to some degree, and even when we're not making conscious hand gestures, the placement of our hands can reveal a lot about how we feel in a given situation. In addition, handshakes and other forms of physical touch can communicate a lot about a person—but it's not always good! This is why it's important to be aware of the handy communication tools we have at the ends of our arms and the many things we express when we use them.

> Talking with your hands is an important part of using body language, but not everyone does it to the same degree. Some people use very few gestures as illustrators in conversations, while others talk with their hands all the time. In addition, people often change the amount and ways they talk with their hands to fit the tone of the conversation.

WHERE SHOULD YOU PUT THEM?

In unfamiliar or stressful circumstances, people sometimes say they don't know what to do with their hands. It can be intimidating to know that the way we use our hands or where we put them while standing still can say something about us. However, by learning what to do with our hands to convey certain feelings, we can be better prepared to present our best self to the world—no matter the circumstances.

Our first reaction when standing around is often to put our hands in our pockets so they have somewhere to be. However, people who hide their hands in their pockets generally appear to be reluctant to communicate. Your hands are such important communication tools that, if you hide them from view, you look as though you are withholding information or unwilling to fully engage in conversation. Out of nervousness or just out of habit, many people hide their hands without realizing they are handicapping themselves by appearing standoffish.

Another hand position that can seem off-putting is what some body language experts call the "fig leaf" pose. In this position, the hands are clasped together and placed in front of the groin area. Humans generally think of their groin as a vulnerable area, so they often try to protect it and cover it without even thinking about it, as is the case with this pose. This protective hand placement can subconsciously signal to others feelings of weakness or fear. It can also indicate a sense of not wanting to be exposed—as if you believe you are inferior to the people around you and want to hide it.

If you want to appear confident, place your hands at your sides. This pose leaves your entire body exposed, which gives off a sense of strength but also makes you look friendly and approachable.

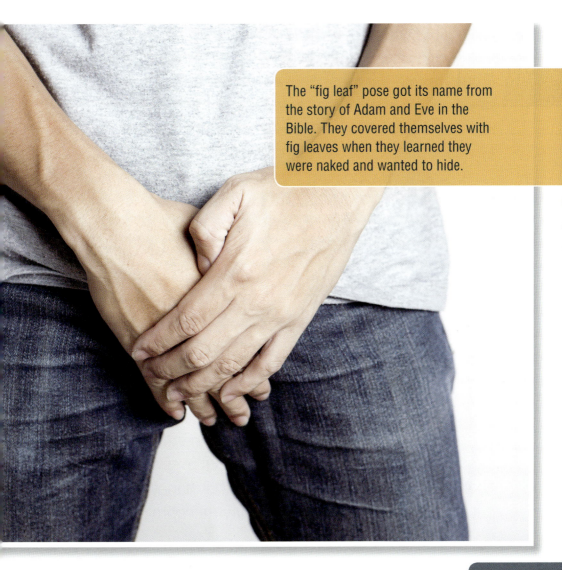

The "fig leaf" pose got its name from the story of Adam and Eve in the Bible. They covered themselves with fig leaves when they learned they were naked and wanted to hide.

TALKING WITH YOUR HANDS

While talking with each other, people often use hand gestures to emphasize a point. One such gesture is the steeple, in which people place the fingertips of both hands together to form an upside-down V shape, or the shape of a church steeple. Used sparingly, the steeple can make you seem sure of yourself and like you know important information. However, too much "steepling" can make people think you're arrogant. This gesture if often used in professional settings by managers or other people speaking to employees of a lower status in an organization. World leaders and other very powerful people frequently use this gesture too.

A more welcoming gesture in professional settings—and especially in public speaking—places the hands a slight distance apart in front of the body, as though they are holding an imaginary ball. Moving your hands up and down a few times in this position helps tell people to pay special attention to what you're saying without making you look like a know-it-all.

The direction your palms are facing while talking can also say a lot about your state of mind, even if you're not completely aware of it yourself. An open-palm gesture makes you seem honest. It shows you have nothing to hide. If you're trying to convince someone of your sincerity, an open palm can help.

A palms-down gesture, on the other hand, can help you cut off a conversation or quiet down a room when you're

A HANDY COMMUNICATION TOOL

Shown here is an example of the steeple hand gesture. It's used by people around the world to convey confidence in what they're saying.

addressing a group. Think about when a politician is speaking to a big crowd of supporters. When they want the cheering crowd to quiet down so they can begin speaking, they often move their hands in a palms-down gesture, as if they're calming them down from the stage.

KEEP YOUR HANDS TO YOURSELF

In America, a handshake is a gesture used in many different settings to greet another person—from a job interview to meeting your prom date's parents. It communicates respect and interest in another person. A firm handshake with a genuine smile and eye contact leaves a good first impression. If your handshake is too weak, it can make you seem insincere, shy, or afraid. If it's too strong, it can make you seem aggressive. Although certain kinds of handshakes can leave the wrong impression, handshakes in general are almost always acceptable and are sometimes expected in certain social situations.

Other touching, though, is far less universally acceptable. If you misspeak with your body language, probably the worst way to do it is through touching someone in an inappropriate way or a way that makes them uncomfortable.

For example, Joe is a new student who is paired with a girl named Nadia in his chemistry class when it's time to assign lab partners. Joe meets Nadia after school to talk about a lab report that is due in a few days. Before they begin discussing the report, though, Nadia suddenly starts crying. Joe asks her what's the matter, and she says her boyfriend just broke up with her. Without thinking, Joe puts his arm around her. Nadia sits up straight, holds her hands up to create a barrier between them, and says, "What do you think you're doing?"

What went wrong? Joe thought he was using his body language to convey a sense of comfort, but instead he made Nadia clearly uncomfortable. Touching is a natural way for a person to provide another with comfort and support, but it is best reserved for people who know each other well and know what the other's boundaries are. Otherwise, it can quickly be misinterpreted. Joe was just trying to make Nadia feel better, and she might have welcomed his touch if they had been longtime friends. However, because Nadia didn't know Joe well, she didn't know what he was communicating through his touch. It made her feel uneasy rather than supported because she thought he might have been trying to get her to date him instead.

In general, you should refrain from touching anyone without their consent. An inappropriate touch might lead to more than a socially awkward moment. It might also get you suspended from school or fired from your job—even if you were just trying to be friendly, nice, or comforting.

For some people, stopping the impulse to touch others is hard. You may have grown up in a family where gestures such as hugging were an important way of communicating love and camaraderie. Keep in mind, though, that others come from families in which people rarely show affection physically. Still others just naturally feel uncomfortable about touching, even touching those closest to them. A safe rule is, if in doubt, keep your hands to yourself.

Setting and Respecting Boundaries

It's important to communicate with others about our boundaries. Boundaries are the ways we define what is and is not acceptable behavior toward us. They're the limits we place on others in terms of how they treat us. Some boundaries are emotional, such as how much you sacrifice to make other people feel happy and to give them what they need. Other boundaries are physical, including who can touch you and what kind of physical contact is acceptable.

It can be hard to set boundaries, especially with friends, romantic partners, and family members. However, it's important for your mental health. For example, if you're not comfortable hugging your dad's new girlfriend, it's important to communicate this clearly. It might feel awkward to set this boundary at first, but it will make you feel better in the long run.

In addition, it's important to listen when other people communicate their boundaries to you. Respecting other people's boundaries is a good way to show them you care about them. If your friend tells you they don't like being touched, it's important to listen to them—even if you're someone who expresses love and care through physical touch. By refraining from hugging them or putting your hand on their shoulder—even when you want to comfort them that way—you're showing them that you value their needs above your wants.

ANXIETY AND ADAPTORS

Another way people use their hands to communicate is through adaptors. They're often less obvious than gesturing while telling a story or touching someone's shoulder to show you care about them, but they still reveal important information. Adaptors often involve people touching parts of their own bodies. Examples include cracking your knuckles, scratching the back of your neck, rubbing your arms, touching your nose or lips, and twirling your hair. People unconsciously use adaptors to comfort themselves when they feel nervous or unsettled.

There are also many other related gestures that involve playing with an object with your hands. Everywhere you look you can see people playing with their jewelry, jiggling their change, or clicking their pen. These activities also help people release nervous energy and therefore make them feel less anxious.

It is hard to stop these gestures. For many people, they are longstanding habits, often ones they are barely aware of. However, even if they do not notice them, other people often do. They typically signal an overall unease. You may think you're projecting an image of a confident, competent person, but if you can't stop drumming on a table with your fingertips, people will instead see an anxious person trying to make themselves feel in control. No matter what the rest of your body language says, these kinds of gestures will broadcast the insecurity hiding behind the confident pose. They're also often distracting to others, especially at school or in professional settings.

Picking at your cuticles or other parts of your hands is a common adaptor.

AWARENESS IS ESSENTIAL

We're often unaware of the adaptors we've been using to make ourselves feel comfortable in stressful situations. You might not know you play with the ponytail holder on your wrist when you feel uneasy until your friend tells you that you do it all the time. You might have no idea you run your hand through your hair when you're anxious until your brother asks why you keep doing that. In fact, you might not have thought about adaptors at all until you read about them right now! However, once you become aware of the gestures you make without meaning to, you can do a better job of trying to control them and, as such, control the messages you share with those around you.

Awareness is an important part of dealing with adaptors, but it's also an important part of all other kinds of body language too—from our awareness of what is and is not appropriate physical contact to our awareness of the gestures we use to communicate confidence when speaking to a crowd. Being aware of our own hand movements helps us communicate clearly with others, and being aware of what others are saying through their hands helps us read between the lines to discover what they really think and feel. That same sense of awareness is important when interpreting the movements of the rest of the body too.

CHAPTER 4
PUTTING THE PIECES TOGETHER

A person's body language involves their whole body—not just their face and their hands. The arms, torso, legs, and even feet communicate important things about what we're thinking and feeling. While the ways we use our face and hands are often the most obvious examples of body language, it's important to take a closer look at the whole body because what someone is saying with their feet might be very different from what they're trying to tell us with their face. By putting all the pieces together, we get the clearest picture of what people are communicating to us.

PUTTING THE PIECES TOGETHER

It's also only when we fully understand how all the parts of our body work together to send messages that we can effectively communicate with others.

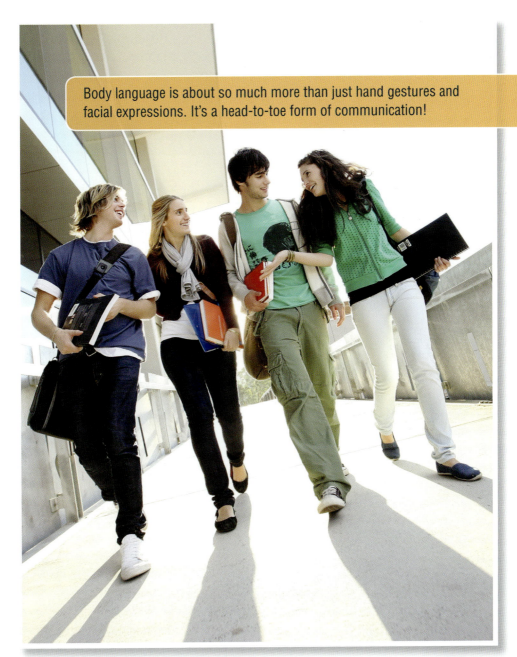

Body language is about so much more than just hand gestures and facial expressions. It's a head-to-toe form of communication!

Watch Your Tone!

Although we use our voice as part of verbal communication, many body language experts actually consider a person's voice to be part of nonverbal communication—not the words it speaks, but the messages its tone conveys. For example, an unchanging tone is so boring that listeners tend to tune it out. A sarcastic tone can convey annoyance, while an excited tone can convey genuine enthusiasm.

The volume and speed of a person's speech can also convey information. If you speak too softly, you come across as weak, but if you speak too loudly, you appear aggressive. Practicing in front of someone you trust and getting their feedback can help you discover if you need to adjust the volume of your voice. In addition, many people talk faster when they're very angry, nervous, or happy. They tend to talk slower when they're frustrated, bored, or sad. To avoid speaking too fast or too slow, take care to insert short pauses after each phrase and longer pauses at the end of each sentence.

To be an effective speaker, also avoid the verbal pause, sometimes known as a verbal crutch. When you use a verbal pause, instead of injecting a brief silence after a phrase, you insert a stand-in word or noise, such as "um," "ah," "like," or "you know." Often, people don't even realize what they are saying or how often they use verbal pauses, but listeners notice. Overusing verbal pauses can make you sound less professional or credible.

PUTTING THE PIECES TOGETHER

To find out if you have a problem with verbal pauses, listen to videos or audio recordings of yourself talking. If you hear a string of "ums" and "likes," start training yourself to replace them with brief, silent pauses. It's a challenging change to make, but it will help your overall effectiveness as a communicator in the long run.

Before you give a speech, record yourself while practicing it. This can help you notice verbal pauses.

UPPER BODY SIGNALS

We communicate a lot through the position of our arms and shoulders. For example, when we hunch our shoulders, we look like we're trying to make ourselves smaller, which can sometimes convey a feeling of weakness or shyness. Another common shoulder movement is a shrug, in which the shoulders lift and the palms face upward. A shrug can show that you don't know what's going on or that you don't care.

Crossing your arms in front of your chest is another way to convey indifference through body language. By doing so, you make your arms a physical barrier between you and others. Crossed arms say that you are closed off and have little desire to communicate. The gesture is likely to make you seem unapproachable and unfriendly.

If you want to give the impression that you are an open and approachable person, it is best to sit with your arms open or to stand with your arms relaxed at your sides. Another confident standing pose is to position your hands on your hips. This is sometimes called the Superman pose or a power pose. It suggests that, just like Superman, you are confident, brave, and ready to jump into action. However, be aware: The Superman pose is hard to pull off successfully. If you do it half-heartedly, you're more likely to look silly than heroic.

PUTTING THE PIECES TOGETHER

Standing in power poses, such as the one shown here, is sometimes said to help people feel more confident in uncomfortable situations. However, some experts disagree with this theory.

READING BODY LANGUAGE

LEARNING FROM THE LEGS

Even your legs can communicate important information. When you're standing, think about if you would be easy to knock over. Standing positions that show feelings of weakness or discomfort include a stance with your legs and feet very close together or standing with one leg crossed in front of the other. In either case, one small shove would be enough to land you on the ground. Contrast these with a firm stance, in which you separate your feet by a few inches and distribute your weight evenly between both of them. This position will make you seem like a powerful person, one who is literally able to stand their ground.

When sitting, some people, especially women, cross their ankles. They might think the pose makes them look polite. However, crossed ankles can actually suggest a person is afraid or wanting to make themselves look smaller. In addition, crossing your legs at the knee while sitting can signal the same thing as crossing your arms over your chest—that you're not approachable or interested in talking. Some people, though, interpret crossed legs as a sign of being interested in the conversation—or as simply a naturally comfortable way of sitting.

On the other end of the spectrum is the figure-four leg position, in which one ankle rests on the knee of the other leg. This makes a person seem

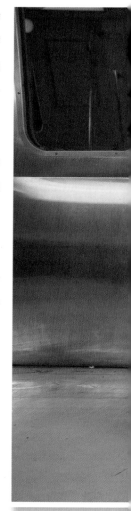

in control and in charge, but, for many people, this position can seem too aggressive. The same can be said of sitting with your legs spread far apart, especially if you're a man. It can be seen as a dominant gesture displaying relaxed confidence, but it's also often seen as a sign of arrogance that makes people, especially women, uncomfortable. For a more neutral, yet confident, leg position while seated, place your feet slightly apart and firmly on the floor.

When a man sits with his legs spread far apart, especially if he's encroaching on a woman's personal space, it's sometimes known as manspreading. Men often don't know they're doing this, but it's good to be aware of this practice because it can make women feel uneasy or annoyed.

PUTTING YOUR BEST FOOT FORWARD

We often forget that even our feet send messages about our feelings. We may think we have complete control over our facial expressions and hand gestures, but if our feet are constantly tapping, we reveal the discomfort we thought was hidden.

Another thing most people pay little attention to is the direction of their feet. Usually, people unconsciously point their feet toward the person who is of the most interest to them. It's as if our feet are showing the direction we'd most like to go in—toward the person or thing we want the most or care the most about. Imagine you are sitting between two friends. Your face is turned toward your friend on the right, but your feet are turned to your friend on the left. You might have inadvertently told your friend on the right that you're much more interested in what your other friend has to say.

POSITIONING YOUR TORSO AND PERSONAL SPACE

The direction of our feet can subconsciously show who we think is most important in a conversation, and the position of our torso can show the same thing. Researchers have stated that people instinctively position their torso so that their belly button points to the person of most interest to them. You can use this knowledge to assure others that you're interested in what they are saying. Just adjust your body so that your belly button is facing squarely in their direction. You can also use this knowledge to show you're ready to finish speaking with someone. Just move your torso at an angle away from them, even as you maintain eye contact with them. Most people will get the hint that the conversation is over.

We often don't think about the position of our torso and what it says about our level of interest in another person and what they're saying. However, the torso is actually an important communication tool!

Another important way of showing interest is to lean forward toward the person you are speaking with. Of course, be careful not to move in too close. That's likely to make other people uncomfortable. Respecting people's personal space is important, and it's often easy to tell from their body language—a slight lean backward or a stiffening of their posture or facial muscles—when we've invaded their space. By the same token, leaning away from someone by slumping in your chair can help break the connection with them and show you're no longer interested in speaking with them.

A VOTE OF CONFIDENCE

Imagine that your school is holding an assembly to present two candidates for student council president. The first candidate walks slowly to the microphone to deliver a speech to convince you to give him your vote. His body is slouched, his shoulders are hunched, and his head is drooping so low that his chin nearly touches his chest. When his speech is over, the second candidate steps onto the stage. She moves swiftly and with purpose. Her back is straight, her shoulders are pushed back, and her head is held high.

Who would you vote for? Based on these descriptions alone, you'd probably say candidate number two. Through her body language, she signaled that she was competent, confident, and determined. She appeared much more able to take on the job of president than the first candidate, whose body seemed to say he was unsure and uncomfortable.

This shows the importance of posture as part of nonverbal communication.

Standing up tall and having an open stance makes you appear confident, while slouching makes you look like you want to hide. Being able to communicate confidence with your body—even when you might not be feeling completely confident—is important. It's also important to be able to recognize nonverbal signs of confidence and discomfort in others because it helps us better navigate social situations and discover what other people want or need. As this student council example shows, we use our entire body to send messages to others, and we can use this knowledge to be the most effective communicators we can be.

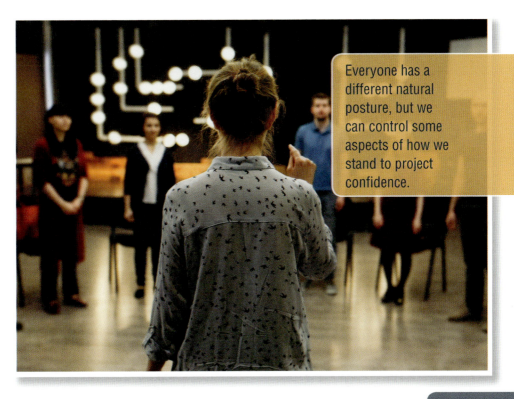

Everyone has a different natural posture, but we can control some aspects of how we stand to project confidence.

MYTHS and facts

Myth
People who don't make eye contact in conversation are lying.

Fact
It's a common misconception that liars are unable to maintain eye contact—so common that many people go out of their way to stare into others' eyes when they are telling lies. The truth is that many people might not look you in the eye for reasons that have nothing to do with what they're saying. Often, they're simply shy or uncomfortable in social situations. People with autism spectrum disorder also have trouble maintaining eye contact.

Myth
Understanding body language can allow you to hide your true feelings easily.

Fact
Some people believe that if they learn enough about body language, they'll be able to use this information to always carefully control the image they present to the world. They think their awareness of things such as facial expressions and posture can help them mask their true feelings whenever they want. However, this is generally untrue. Microexpressions are made even by the most self-aware body language experts, giving away the truth about how they feel if someone is paying close attention. Understanding body language can help us more clearly communicate with others, but it's at its best as a communication tool when it's being used to show the truth.

PUTTING THE PIECES TOGETHER

Myth
A single gesture can tell you all you need to know about how someone is feeling.

Fact
Making assumptions about anyone's true feelings, especially based on only one gesture, is not a very good idea. It's better to have more information, either from other aspects of their body language or from what they're communicating verbally. Some gestures, such as rubbing the back of the neck, can mean that a person is anxious. Then again, maybe it just means the person has a sore or itchy neck, which is why they're touching it.

As this example suggests, trying to read what someone is thinking and feeling through body language is tricky. Don't draw conclusions from a single gesture. Instead, you should study their entire body to see if it's sending you a complete message. If the person rubbing their neck is also clicking their pen constantly and biting their lip, it's a clearer indication that they're nervous or uncomfortable. However, if other than the neck rub, they seem calm and collected, maybe you were jumping to conclusions when you decided they had a bad case of nerves.

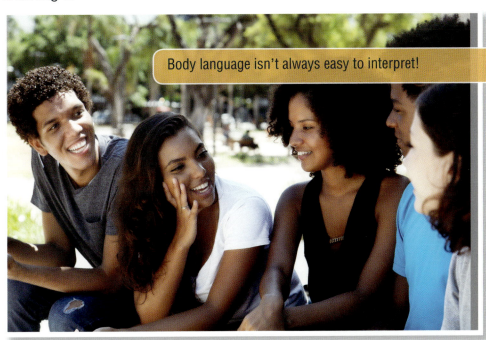
Body language isn't always easy to interpret!

CHAPTER 5
BODY LANGUAGE IN ACTION

Understanding body language is an essential communication skill that helps us see others—and ourselves—more clearly. For example, observing your best friend's body language can help you figure out when they're sad but trying to hide it. A strong knowledge of body language can also help you when you meet new people. If the new student in your class has a relaxed, open posture and a smile that reaches their eyes, you'll know they're most likely feeling confident and ready to make new friends. However, if they're fidgeting with their earrings and standing with their legs crossed, you'll know they're most likely feeling nervous and in need of some help introducing themselves.

When you take control of your own body language, you'll be able to more effectively communicate with everyone around you. Although there are some aspects of body language, such as microexpressions and other instant physical reactions, that are impossible to fully control, we can shape many aspects of our nonverbal communication style to make sure the messages we're sending out are exactly the ones we want other people to receive. It takes work to put our understanding of body language into action, but it's worth the extra effort.

We use our body language to communicate with others at home, at school, at work, and everywhere else we go.

WHAT OTHERS ARE SAYING

Many people who want to study body language want to learn how to read the body language of others. Reading other people's body language, however, is fairly hard. One gesture doesn't have a single meaning. If a person's hands are tightly wrapped around their arms, it could signal that the person is closed off and not interested in having a conversation, or it could simply mean they're cold.

If you want to interpret someone's body language, it's helpful to know what they look like when they're feeling calm so you can contrast those gestures with ones that might signal a change in their emotional state. For example, imagine getting called to the principal's office. She's asking you a lot of questions about your friends, and you don't really know what she wants from you. You notice that the principal normally sits leaning back in her chair. However, at one point when you're talking, she leans forward. That deviation suggests that whatever you were saying at that particular moment is the information she wanted.

Even if you study someone's body language closely, it's important to remember that it's just one tool that can be used to help make communication more effective. It's not a way to learn everyone's secret thoughts or feelings. Making assumptions about a person based on their body language is a normal part of human behavior, but it's good to follow up those assumptions with verbal communication to learn more about someone. In some cases, people are unaware of the signals they're sending, and treating them differently—especially poorly—because of what you think their body language is saying can cause hurt feelings and misunderstandings.

THE SIGNALS WE SEND

We all have moments of being unaware of the signals we're sending through our body language. That's why learning about body language is such an important part of improving our own communication style. When we study our own body language with the knowledge of what various expressions, gestures, and stances say to others about our state of mind, we can learn to communicate more clearly and have a stronger sense of self-awareness.

When we study our own body language, we often discover bad habits that can give people the wrong impression of us from our gestures or posture alone. You'll likely find these habits difficult to break, but it is possible to change them.

You can ask a friend or family member to point out when you use adaptors such as playing with your jewelry or hair. This can help you break that habit. You can also reduce the negative messages sent through your body language by changing certain things around you. If you always shove your hands into your pockets and don't want people to think you're not friendly, try wearing clothes without them.

If you really want to develop control over your body language, you need to do more than just break old bad habits, though. You need to cultivate new ones that send confident messages. Doing so can be tricky, though. For example, if you began punctuating everything you say with steeple hands, your friends will likely start looking at you strangely. You won't look effortlessly confident because the gesturing will seem forced.

It's better to take it slow. Try using steeple hands once to emphasize an important point in a conversation. Think about whether it feels natural to you. More important, check the reaction of the people you're talking with. Do they seem to be reacting positively to it?

Adopting new body language habits will be difficult at first. When you're gesturing consciously instead of subconsciously, it will probably feel odd, but with some practice, you will become comfortable using new gestures or standing or sitting in new ways. In time, they may even become second nature to you.

CREATING A CONNECTION

Working toward a clearer and more confident use of body language in your everyday life starts with one basic question: What goal do I want my body language to achieve?

In many situations, the answer is simple. You want your body language to help create a

BODY LANGUAGE IN ACTION

Friends can be a big help in the development of good body language habits and the changing of bad ones. However, pointing out adaptors or other signals of discomfort should only be done if a friend asks you to. Otherwise, it can make them feel uncomfortable. It should also always be done in a kind, empathetic way.

Evaluating Yourself

Asking friends or family members to assist you in improving the clarity of your body language is very helpful. However, it's also important to study your own body language and what it's communicating about your thoughts and feelings. One way to study your own body language is by looking at videos of yourself. You can even ask a friend to film you in conversation or while giving a speech.

A mirror can also help you evaluate your nonverbal communication. Stand before a full-length mirror, and close your eyes. Think about a time you felt nervous or afraid. Open your eyes, and examine your body and your expression. Close your eyes again, and think about a time you felt confident and in control. Then, open your eyes, and take note of how your body language has changed.

A mirror can also help you see how much more confident you look when you stand tall, pull your shoulders back, and position your weight evenly on both feet. You can even try out new hand gestures or practice certain facial expressions using a mirror first—especially before an event like a big speech or job interview. This can help you see what they look like and what kind of signals they're communicating before you use them in front of others. Do they look forced, or do they seem natural? A mirror is one of the best tools to use to answer this question.

positive connection between you and the person or people you're interacting with. Central to that is making a good first impression. When you are introduced to people, shake hands firmly (but not with too much force), if appropriate. Maintain steady but not constant eye contact, and try to smile genuinely while matching their energy level. If they seem excited, it's good for your body language to convey excitement too. If they have a calmer energy, then work to match your body language to that by making fewer gestures. This helps the other person feel more comfortable.

Matching or mimicking the body language of another person is known as mirroring, and it can help create a sense of connection and empathy between people. Seeing one's own gestures repeated is comforting. It also subtly suggests that you and the other person are on the same wavelength. Of course, if you take the mimicking too far, this body language strategy will backfire. It could look and feel very calculated, which can immediately make you seem fake. It could even make it seem like you're making fun of the other person. It's good to mirror some gestures—which often happens subconsciously anyway—but not all of them to make the interaction feel more natural.

Once the conversation gets going, slightly leaning toward the other person will signal that you're interested in what they're saying. Also, when a person says something you agree with, a firm, single nod will show that you're on the same page. Maintaining eye contact and keeping your posture open can help build connection throughout a conversation.

READING BODY LANGUAGE

Body language is the key to making a strong first impression—whether that's in a job interview, at an internship, on a first date, or while meeting a new classmate.

PROFESSIONAL POSTURES

Sometimes your goal in a conversation is to create a warm, positive connection with another person. Other times it can be to convince people that you are a serious, competent person. For example, in all college and job interviews, giving this impression is just as important as anything you've written on your application. This is also a big part of making a speech or giving a presentation.

Body language is one of the most important tools you have to show others that you're competent and confident.

10 Great Questions
TO ASK A TEACHER

1. What are the basic building blocks of body language?

2. How much of our communication is nonverbal?

3. How early do humans start using body language to communicate?

4. Does a single gesture always have the same meaning?

5. Why do gestures and expressions differ around the world?

6. Can body language reveal that someone is lying?

7. Is it possible for people to change their body language when so much of it is subconscious?

8. How can we improve our body language so we appear more engaged in conversations and more willing to communicate with others?

9. Can practicing confident body language help us feel more confident?

10. How do certain mental or physical differences impact the use and understanding of body language?

Stand tall with your head up and shoulders back, and when you sit, be sure to maintain this open posture. Keeping your arms and hands visible and open will help you seem truthful and like you have nothing to hide.

In a formal conversation, be careful about adaptors, which will immediately show any nervousness you're feeling. Also, try not to make any gesture unless it has a concrete purpose, such as emphasizing a point.

When making a speech, make eye contact with people in the audience early on. If you don't make that early eye contact, you run the risk of losing their attention for the entire presentation. Simple, direct, open-palm hand gestures can help you alert the audience to your most important points. Take care not to bring your hands above your chin, or your gesturing will seem more like flailing. Practicing your speech with the gestures you want to use in front of a mirror can help you project the most confident body image possible when it's time to actually address your audience.

SMALL CHANGES MAKE A BIG DIFFERENCE

When you start practicing interactions in front of a mirror and noticing your body language, you'll most likely notice an important connection between how you look and how you feel. When you stand up tall and use direct gestures, you'll feel more confident. On the other hand, when you cross your arms in front of you, you'll feel less open. The way we move often plays a big part in how we feel.

BODY LANGUAGE IN ACTION

This reveals what can be so powerful about understanding and utilizing your body language to the best of your ability. While working to change how others see you, you can also change how you see yourself. For example, if you mindfully adopt a more open, confident stance when you feel shy or insecure, you might find that you feel better about yourself and are more welcoming to others. Just by making small changes to how you carry yourself, you might open yourself up to new friends and new possibilities in many areas of your life.

Body language is even important when giving a virtual presentation or speech. A virtual audience is still an audience!

GLOSSARY

ancestor One of the people from whom a person is descended.

calculated Carefully planned for a particular and often improper purpose.

circumstance An event or situation that you cannot control.

competent Able to do something well.

comprehensible Able to be understood.

concrete Involving specifics rather than general ideas or qualities.

consciously Done with awareness.

contempt A feeling that someone or something is not worthy of any respect or approval.

convey To make known.

cultivate To develop something under conditions you can control.

deviation An action, behavior, or condition that is different from what is usual or expected.

encroach To go beyond the usual or proper limits.

evaluate To judge the value or condition of something in a careful and thoughtful way.

evolution The theory that various kinds of existing animals and plants have come from kinds that existed in the past.

flare To open or spread outward.

gesture A movement of the body that shows or emphasizes an idea or a feeling. Also, to make such a movement.

impulse A sudden or strong desire to do something.

inadvertently Not intended or planned.

indicate To show or suggest something.

internship An educational or training program that gives experience for a career.

intimacy A state marked by emotional closeness.

misconception A wrong or mistaken idea.

naturalist A person who studies plants and animals as they live in nature.

posture The way in which your body is positioned when you are sitting or standing.

pupil The opening of the iris through which light enters the eye.

stance A way of standing.

theory An idea suggested or presented as possibly true but that is not known or proven to be true.

torso The human body except for the head, neck, arms, and legs.

FOR MORE INFORMATION

Berkeley Psychophysiology Lab
University of California, Berkeley
2121 Berkeley Way
Berkeley, CA 94720
(510) 643-8952
Website: bpl.berkeley.edu/
The Berkeley Psychophysiology Lab analyzes the connections between emotions and physical processes, including the movement of facial muscles responsible for expressions.

Girls Inc.
120 Wall Street, 18th Floor
New York, NY 10005
(212) 509-2000
Website: girlsinc.org/
Girls Inc. is devoted to the development of the next generation of female leaders, and its mission includes fostering the development of confidence and strong interpersonal communication skills in young women.

Goldwin-Meadow Laboratory
University of Chicago, Department of Psychology
5848 South University Avenue
Chicago, IL 60637
(773) 702-1562
Website: voices.uchicago.edu/goldinmeadowlab/
This laboratory, which is part of the University of Chicago's Department of Psychology, is devoted to studying nonverbal communication, especially gestures.

International Communication Association
1500 21st Street NW
Washington, DC 20036
(202) 955-1444
Website: www.icahdq.org/
The International Communication Association works to support research into all forms of communication around the world.

International Society of Gesture Studies
University of Texas at Austin
Department of Communication Studies
1 University Station
Austin, TX 78712
Email: isgs@gesturestudies.com
Website: gesturestudies.com/
This organization is the only international scholarly association dedicated to the study of gestures.

National Communication Association
1765 N Street NW
Washington, DC 20036
(202) 464-4622
Website: www.natcom.org
The National Communication Association studies all forms, modes, and consequences of communication, including nonverbal communication.

FOR FURTHER READING

Bowden, Mark. *Winning Body Language*. New York, NY: McGraw-Hill, 2010.

Brehove, Aaron. *Body Language: Techniques on Interpreting Nonverbal Cues in the World and Workplace*. Guilford, CT: Knack, 2011.

Brian, Rachel. *Respect: Consent, Boundaries, and Being in Charge of You*. London, UK: Wren & Rook, 2020.

Currie-McGhee, L. K. *Getting a Job*. San Diego, CA: ReferencePoint Press, Inc., 2020.

Ellsberg, Michael. *The Power of Eye Contact*. New York, NY: HarperPaperbacks, 2010.

Fitzsimons, Kate. *The Teen's Guide to Social Skills: Practical Advice for Building Empathy, Self-Esteem, & Confidence*. Emeryville, CA: Rockridge Press, 2021.

German, Kathleen M. *Principles of Public Speaking*. New York, NY: Routledge, 2020.

Hartley, Gregory, and Maryann Karinch. *The Body Language Handbook*. Pompton Plains, NJ: Career Press, 2010.

Jackson, Donna M. *Every Body's Talking: What We Say Without Words.* Minneapolis, MN: Twenty-First Century Books, 2014.

Johnson, Robin. *Above and Beyond with Communication*. New York, NY: Crabtree Publishing Company, 2017.

Kay, Katty, Claire Shipman, and JillEllyn Riley. *The Confidence Code for Girls: Taking Risks, Messing Up, & Becoming Your Amazingly Imperfect, Totally Powerful Self*. New York, NY: Harper, 2018.

Knowles, Sue, Bridie Gallagher, and Hannah Bromley. *My Intense Emotions Handbook: Manage Your Emotions and Connect Better with Others*. London, UK: Jessica Kingsley Publishers, 2021.

Rand, Casey. *Communication*. Chicago, IL: Raintree, 2012.

Randy, Charles. *Communication Skills.* Broomall, PA: Mason Crest, 2019.

Reeves, Diane Lindsey, Connie Hansen, and Ruth Bennett. *Communication*. Ann Arbor, MI: Cherry Lake Publishing, 2021.

Santoro, Marisa. *Own Your Authority: Follow Your Instincts, Radiate Confidence and Communicate as a Leader People Trust*. New York, NY: McGraw Hill Education, 2021.

Sayler, Sharon. *What Your Body Says and How to Master the Message.* Hoboken, NJ: John Wiley & Sons, 2010.

Skeen, Michelle. *Communication Skills for Teens: How to Listen, Express & Connect for Success.* Oakland, CA: Instant Help Books, 2016.

Sterling, Lindsey. *The Social Survival Guide for Teens on the Autism Spectrum: How to Make Friends and Navigate Your Emotions*. Emeryville, CA: Rockridge Press, 2020.

Swift, Kelly. *Life Skills*. New York, NY: DK Publishing, 2021.

INDEX

A

adaptors, as category of body movement, 15, 17, 18, 19, 41, 42, 61, 63, 68

affect displays, as category of body movement, 14, 15, 19

Afghanistan, 16

aggressiveness, 16, 27, 38, 46, 51

anger, 26, 46
    as universal facial expression, 23

anxiety, 15, 17, 18, 26, 41, 43, 57

arms/crossing arms, 13, 38, 41, 44, 48, 50, 60, 68

autism spectrum disorder (ASD), and nonverbal communication, 28, 56

B

body, direction of, 6, 13

body language
    and babies, 11, 12, 19, 28
    controlling/changing, 17–18, 61–62, 64
    different meanings in different countries, 16
    as earliest form of communication, 11–12
    explanation of, 6, 8
    as field of study, 9
    interpreting, 6, 9, 28, 39, 43, 50, 57, 60–61

body movements, five categories of, 13–15

boredom, 26, 27, 29, 46

boundaries, setting and respecting, 40

C

change/coins, playing with, 41

confidence, 6, 26, 27, 35, 37, 41, 48, 49, 51, 54, 55, 58, 61, 62, 64, 66, 68, 69

contempt, as universal emotion, 24

D

Darwin, Charles, 9

disgust, as universal facial expression, 23

E

Ekman, Paul, 13, 22, 24

embarrassment, 26

emblems, as category of body movement, 14, 18, 19

emotions, 9, 13, 14, 17, 20, 22–24, 25, 26, 40, 60

England, 16

excitement, 6, 14, 26, 46, 65

Expression of the Emotions in Man and Animals, The, 9

eye contact, 4, 6, 8, 13, 16, 26–27, 28, 30, 38, 56, 65, 68

F

Facial Action Coding System (FACS), 9

facial expressions, 6, 8, 9, 11, 14, 17, 20–21, 23, 29, 30, 45, 52, 64

  eye contact, 4, 6, 8, 13, 16, 26–27, 28, 30, 38, 56, 65, 68

  faking, 21, 24–25, 56

  and people with ASD, 28

  smiling/smiles, 11, 12, 13, 17, 25, 26, 38, 58, 65

  universal emotions and expressions, 22–24

fear/being afraid, 24, 35, 38, 50, 64

  as universal facial expression, 23

feet, looking down at, 6

feet and legs, position of, 8, 50–51, 52

"fig leaf" hand pose, 34–35

figure-four leg position, 50–51

first impressions, body language and, 13, 38, 65, 66

France, 16

Friesen, Wallace V., 13

frowning/frowns, 6, 11, 14

G

Greece, 16

H

hair, playing with, 18, 41, 43, 61

hand gestures, 6, 8, 11, 16, 22, 32, 36–43, 45, 52, 64

  adaptors, 15, 17, 18, 41, 42, 61, 63, 68

  being aware of, 43

  "fig leaf" pose, 34–35

  hand positions, 34–35, 36

  OK hand gesture, 16, 18

  open-palm gesture, 36, 68

  palms-down gesture, 36–37

  shaking hands, 27, 32, 38, 65

  "steeple" pose, 36, 37, 62

  thumbs-up gesture, 15, 16

  touching others, 38–39, 40

hand waving, 16, 18

happiness, 12, 17, 24, 25, 26, 27, 40, 46

  as universal facial expression, 23

head movements, 8, 11, 22, 29–30

head position, 29

hugging, 39, 40

I

illustrators, as category of body movement, 14, 18, 19

insecurity, 41, 69

interviews, 4, 38, 64, 66–68

Iran, 16

J

jewelry, playing with, 15, 41, 58, 61

K

knuckle cracking, 41

L

language barriers, and importance of nonverbal communication, 7, 11, 16

legs and feet, position of, 8, 50–51, 52

looking away, 14

M

manspreading, 51

microexpressions, 24, 56, 59

mirroring, 65

N

nail biting, 17, 18

neck rubbing/scratching, 15, 41, 57

nervousness, 15, 34, 46, 57, 59, 64, 68

Nigeria, 16

nodding, 11, 14, 16, 22, 29, 65

nonverbal communication, explanation of, 6

O

OK hand gesture, 16, 18

P

pen clicking, 15, 41, 57

personal space, 8, 54

posture, 6, 54, 55, 56, 58, 61, 65, 68

power pose, 38, 49

pupils, dilating of, 17

R

regulators, as category of body movement, 14, 19

respect, 27, 38, 40, 54

S

sadness, 6, 24, 26, 46, 58
  as universal facial expression, 23

shaking hands, 27, 32, 38, 65

shoulders, 40, 41, 48, 54, 64, 68

shrugging, 48

shyness, 6, 26, 29, 38, 48, 56, 69

sincerity, 36, 38

slouching, 4, 6, 54, 55

smiling/smiles, 11, 12, 13, 17, 25, 26, 38, 58, 65

space between people/personal space, 8, 54

speeches, 47, 54, 64, 66, 68, 69

"steeple" hand pose, 36, 37, 62

Superman pose, 48

surprise, as universal facial expression, 23

T

tension, 17, 26

thumbs-up gesture, 15, 16

tone of voice, 12, 46–47

torso, position of, 52–54

Turkey, 16

U

upper body signals, 48

V

verbal communication, explanation of, 4

verbal pause/crutch, 46–47

PHOTO CREDITS

Cover MilanMarkovic78/Shutterstock.com; p. 5 garetsworkshop/Shutterstock.com; p. 7 Syda Productions/Shutterstock.com; pp. 8, 20, 32, 44, 58 en-owai/Shutterstock.com; p. 10 Olimpik/Shutterstock.com; p. 12 takayuki/Shutterstock.com; pp. 15, 23 Prostock-studio/Shutterstock.com; p. 18 True Touch Lifestyle/Shutterstock.com; p. 21 Veja/Shutterstock.com; pp. 22, 24–25 G-Stock Studio/Shutterstock.com; pp. 26–27 eakkachai halang/Shutterstock.com; pp. 30–31 FXQuadro/Shutterstock.com; p. 33 WAYHOME studio/Shutterstock.com; pp. 34–35 CHAjAMP/Shutterstock.com; pp. 36–37 Mangostar/Shutterstock.com; pp. 42–43 Lolostock/Shutterstock.com; p. 45 sirtravelalot/Shutterstock.com; pp. 47, 66, 69 fizkes/Shutterstock.com; p. 49 sanneberg/Shutterstock.com; pp. 50–51 Kawin Ounprasertsuk/Shutterstock.com; p. 53 wavebreakmedia/Shutterstock.com; p. 55 jonnyslav/Shutterstock.com; p. 57 Daniel M. Ernst/Shutterstock.com; p. 59 Rawpixel.com/Shutterstock.com; pp. 62–63 AS photostudio/Shutterstock.com.

Designer: Michael Flynn; Editor: Greg Roza